THE
GREEDY RABBIT
AND
OTHER STORIES

The Greedy Rabbit

and Other Stories

by
ENID BLYTON

Illustrated by
RENE CLOKE and BRIAN HOSKIN

AWARD PUBLICATIONS

For further information on Enid Blyton please visit *www.blyton.com*

ISBN 978-1-84135-428-6

First published by Award Publications Limited 1999
This edition first published 2005

Published by Award Publications Limited,
The Old Riding School, The Welbeck Estate,
Worksop, Nottinghamshire, S80 3LR

13 7

Printed in the United Kingdom

CONTENTS

1

Snubby's Tail

Snubby was a fat little guinea-pig. He was perfectly tame and lived in a nice hutch in Leslie's garden. He had plenty to eat, and a nice soft bed to lie on, so he was very happy.

At least he was very happy till he got out of his cage one night and met Frisky the squirrel, who was scampering about in the moonlight, having a fine game.

'Hallo there!' said Frisky in surprise. 'What sort of an animal are you? I've never seen a creature like you before.'

'Oh,' said Snubby, 'well, I don't really know what I am. I am called Snubby.'

'Snubby!' said Frisky. 'Well, I've never heard of snubbies before! So you

are a snubby? Let's have a look at you.'

He bounded all round Snubby and then roared with laughter.

'You've come out without your tail!' he said. 'Where is it?'

'My tail!' said Snubby astonished. 'Oh dear! Haven't I got one on?'

'No,' said Frisky. 'What have you done with it? Have you lost it?'

'I must have,' said Snubby sadly, looking at Frisky's beautiful bushy tail.

'We'll ask people if they have seen it,' said Frisky, and he took hold of

8

Snubby's front paw and went off with him. 'Look! There's Mrs. Quack! Let's ask her!'

They went up to a large white duck who was busy diving for food in a nearby pond. She stared at Snubby in surprise when she saw him, for she had never seen such a creature before.

'This is a snubby,' said Frisky. 'He has lost his tail. Look!'

Mrs. Quack looked. 'Dear, dear!' she said. 'So he has. What a pity!' She wagged her own feathery tail to make

9

sure she had it, and Snubby did wish he had one like hers.

'I haven't seen the snubby's tail,' she said. 'But Willie the dog is somewhere about, hunting rats. He may have seen it.'

So Snubby, Frisky and Mrs. Quack went off together to look for Willie the dog.

He was hunting rats, and had his head down a hole. He had a fine long tail that wagged when the others spoke to him. Snubby did wish he had a tail like that.

'Hallo, hallo!' said Willie, pulling his head out of the hole and looking at the others. 'What's all this? Whatever is this curious creature?'

'It's a snubby,' said Mrs. Quack and Frisky together. 'Isn't he curious! He hasn't a tail – look! He must have lost it. We wondered if you had seen it.'

'No, I haven't,' said Willie. 'But there's an old rat-tail he can have if he likes.'

'No, thank you!' said Snubby at once. 'I'm not going to have a tail like that! I want one like Frisky's – or like Mrs. Quack's, or yours, Willie!'

'Oh, well!' said Willie, 'if you're going to be so particular, I'm afraid I can't help you! I haven't seen your lost tail!'

'Don't be cross, Willie,' said Frisky. 'You are a clever dog – just think hard for a minute and see if you can think of some way to get back the snubby's tail!'

So Willie thought hard. Then he wuffed and said: 'Of course! There's the wishing-well! If we can get old Mother Turnabout to come with us to the well, she can get Snubby's tail for us!'

So off they all went to Mother Turnabout's. She was knitting by the fire, and was most astonished to see Snubby, Frisky, Mrs. Quack and Willie walking in at the door.

'Bless us all!' she cried. 'What's this? Now what have you come for at this time of night?'

'Please, Mother Turnabout, will you come with us to the wishing-well, and wish back the little snubby's lost tail for us?' begged Frisky. 'He lost it coming along to-night, and he is so miserable without it.'

'I've never heard of a snubby before,' said Mother Turnabout, peering at

Snubby's Tail

Snubby through her spectacles. 'Funny little chap, he looks! Well, I'll come – but mind you, creatures – I shall want an egg from you, Mrs. Quack – a score of nuts from you, Frisky – and you'll please to guard my house for me for a week, Willie. As for you, little snubby thing, I don't know if you lay eggs or what you do – but when you've got your tail back, you can repay me in some way!'

They all went out of the door and made their way to the old wishing-well in Mother Turnabout's garden. She

14

took a shiny green stone, and dropped
it down the well. Then she spoke softly.
  'Well, wishing-well, are you listening?
Bring back the tail of the little snubby!'
  She let down a bucket into the water,
and then slowly pulled it up again. She
put her hand into the bucket to get out

15

the tail she expected to find there.

'How very strange!' she said at last. 'There is no tail here! This is the first time that the wishing-well has ever failed to grant a wish! I must let the bucket down again!'

Down it went again – and up it came again – but there was no tail there! Mother Turnabout grunted, and walked back to her cottage, sad and puzzled.

All the creatures followed her, quite frightened. The old dame sat down in a chair and frowned.

'I can't make it out!' she said. 'Why didn't it grant my wish? Surely, oh surely, the magic hasn't gone out of my wishing-well!'

She stood up and went to the door. She called loudly: 'Cinders, Cinders, Cinders!'

A big black cat with green eyes came bounding up. He was astonished to see Mother Turnabout's visitors, and he spat rudely at the dog.

'Cinders!' said the old dame. 'I wished for the tail of this little snubby

16

to come back, for he lost it this evening
– and it didn't come back!'

'Then he didn't lose it,' said the cat.

'But he must have!' cried Mrs. Quack,
Willie and Frisky. 'He hasn't got it on!'

'Let me see,' said the cat. So Snubby
came forward and then turned himself
slowly round backwards. Sure enough,
he had no tail.

But Cinders looked at him closely –
and then he began to laugh, showing
all his sharp white teeth.

'What's the matter?' cried everyone.

17

'Why, that's a guinea-pig and they don't have tails!' said the cat. 'He didn't lose his tail – he never had one! Ho, ho, ho! What a joke!'

'You said he was a snubby!' cried Mother Turnabout angrily, to Frisky.

'He said he was!' cried Frisky.

'I didn't! I said my name was Snubby, and so it is!' cried Snubby quite frightened. All the animals looked so fierce that he made up his mind to run – and out of the door he went as fast as his four little legs could carry him.

'After him!' cried Willie – and out they all went, leaving Mother Turnabout in her chair, feeling very glad indeed to think that the magic hadn't gone out of her well after all!

Snubby hid under a bush and Mrs. Quack, Willie and Frisky ran by. Then out he crept and ran back to his hutch as fast as he could. How glad he was to be there once more! He shut the door with his own snubby nose and was pleased to hear the click that told him it was latched. He was safe!

'I don't want a stupid tail!' he thought. 'If you have a tail, you have to keep a wag in it, and that would be such a nuisance. I'm lucky to have no tail!'

And he went to sleep, and dreamed that Mother Turnabout had stolen Frisky's tail, and Willie's tail and Mrs. Quack's as well, and had put them all into her best Sunday hat. How he laughed when he woke up! Funny little Snubby!

2

The Shivery Snowman

One cold winter's day, when the snow was very thick on the ground, two children ran into the fields by Pixie Hill.

'Let's build a snowman!' they cried. 'It would be such fun! There is plenty of snow.'

So they built a snowman – not very large, because they really hadn't much time. He had a nice round head, a short thick body, two arms, and no legs at all, but just big feet sticking out at the bottom. They put a pair of old raggedy gloves on his hands, and on his head, a dirty old hat, which they found in a nearby hedge. They gave him stones down his front for buttons – and two black stones for eyes. His nose was a bent twig and so was his mouth.

Really, he looked very fine when they had finished with him – quite real, in fact! The children were delighted and they danced round him, shouting loudly.

'We've made a man of snow, of snow, hie-diddle-hie, hie-diddle-o, we've made a man of snow, of snow!'

Then the boy looked at his watch and found that it was almost dinner-time, so off scurried the two children over the snowy fields, back to their home.

The snowman was left alone. A robin flew down and perched on his hat. 'Trilla, trilla,' he said to the snowman. 'How do you feel, Mister Snowman, out here in the snowy field. Are you lonely?'

The snowman made a little shivery sound. He wasn't quite sure where his voice grew, but he found it at last.

'No, I'm not lonely,' he said. 'I haven't had time to be yet.'

'Wait till it gets dark, and the birds are gone to bed,' sang the robin. 'You may be lonely then. I will tell the little folk who live in Pixie Hill to come and talk to you if you like. You may be frightened in the dark.'

The snowman looked all round him with his black stone eyes. It seemed a very nice world to him. He enjoyed himself very much that day, but when the afternoon changed to evening, he didn't like it at all. He could see nothing then, and he couldn't understand it. He began to feel very frightened indeed.

Suddenly a little voice spoke near to him, and he saw a tiny lantern.

'Good evening, snowman,' said the voice. 'The robin told us about you. We have come to keep you company. Are you lonely?'

The snowman blinked in the light of the lantern. He saw a small pixie holding it – and behind him were about twelve others, all dressed in fleecy overcoats, with pointed fur caps on their heads.

'Good evening,' said the snowman, trying to smile, with his bent twig mouth. 'Yes – I was feeling a bit lonely, and a bit frightened too, you know. It is very pleasant to see you.'

The pixies sat down in a ring, and looked at the snowman kindly. They were good-hearted little creatures, always ready to do anyone a good turn. One of them put out his hand and touched the snowman. Then he gave a scream.

'Ooooh! How cold you are! Poor, poor thing! If I felt as cold as you I should cry and cry!'

All the pixies felt the snowman in turn and shrieked in horror to feel how cold he was. The snowman began to feel that he must indeed be cold, and he shivered from head to foot. The pixies saw him and all began talking at once.

'What can we do for him? Poor, poor creature! Here he is out in the cold, open field, with a frosty wind blowing, and not even an overcoat on!'

'We could build a little fence round him of twigs,' said one pixie, running to the hedge at once.

'And I have an old hot water bottle at home I could lend him,' said another, running to Pixie Hill in a trice.

'And I could bake him two hot potatoes to eat!' said a third, and ran off too.

The others sat and looked at the snowman who was now shivering so much that his hat went all crooked.

'We will make him a nice little fire to warm himself by,' said the other pixies, out of the kindness of their hearts. So they set to work to collect dry leaves

and sticks and by the time the other three pixies had come back with the little hot water bottle, and the two hot potatoes, they had made a fine crackling fire, round which they all crowded - for it was certainly a very cold night indeed!

Two other pixies had built a splendid fence round the snowman, and the wind did not feel nearly so cold to his back. He was most grateful. It was lovely to be fussed over like this!

Just then a big white shape swooped out of the night and the pixies screamed in fright. But it was only the barn owl

The Shivery Snowman

come to see what all the noise was about. When he saw the snowman and the pixies, with their fire and fence and all the rest, he hooted and screeched with laughter.

'What's the matter?' cried the pixies crossly.

'Matter enough!' said the old owl, with another screech. 'There's such a thing as being too kind, you know! That snowman will be sorry for himself in the morning! Too much kindness is simply foolishness!'

With another loud screech he flew off into the night, leaving the pixies talking angrily about him to one another.

'Nasty old thing!' said one. 'Trying

to make out that we are too kind! How can kindness ever be foolish!'

'Don't listen to him,' said the snowman, who was enjoying all the fussing and petting very much indeed. 'Where is that hot water bottle, pixie?'

What a time he had! One pixie popped the hot potatoes into his mouth and he swallowed them down. Another gave him the hot water bottle to hug to his middle with both his gloved hands – and all the rest heaped up the fire and made him as warm as possible.

He suddenly began to feel very sleepy. There was a funny feeling in his middle too, where he was holding the nice hot water bottle. He thought he really must nod off and go to sleep just for a few minutes.

The pixies went on talking to him. When he didn't answer they were surprised.

'Poor thing, he's gone to sleep!' said one, holding up his lantern, and seeing that the snowman's head had slid a little forward. 'Don't let's disturb him with our chatter. Let's heap up the fire and creep away quietly. He will sleep soundly all night, and wake up well and happy to-morrow.'

So all the pixies crept away, taking their small lanterns with them, and

leaving the fire crackling away at the snowman's feet.

The snowman tried to wake up – but he couldn't. He really felt very funny indeed – much too hot, in fact! The barn owl came sweeping by again, on his great silent wings, and let out a screech of laughter when he saw the old snowman standing all humped up – looking really much smaller now. But the snowman didn't even wake up when the owl screeched.

The night passed. The winter sun rose red in the sky. The pixies came running out to say good morning to the snowman – but where, oh, where had he gone?

He wasn't there! He simply wasn't there! Only the little twig fence stood where they had built it – and some black ashes lay where the fire had been. Hidden in the snow beneath was the hot water bottle, but the pixies didn't know it had fallen there. They were very much upset.

'He's walked off!' they cried in dismay. 'Oh, how horrid of him! He's taken our hot water bottle, too! Would you believe it – after all our kindness! He's quite, quite gone!'

They kicked down the little fence they had made, and stamped on the ashes. They were very angry indeed.

'Listen!' said one pixie suddenly. 'I can hear children coming! Quick! Run!'

They scampered off – and soon up came the two children who had made the snowman the day before. They had brought spades with them this time, and meant to build an even bigger snowman.

'Where's our snowman that we built

yesterday?' cried the boy, in astonishment.

'He's disappeared!' said the girl, looking all about the field. 'I know quite well this is where we made him yesterday, John.'

'But how can he have disappeared?' wondered the boy. 'It's been very cold and frosty – he ought still to be here. Whatever has happened to him? I do so wish we knew!'

They would have known if they had heard the old barn owl that night, screeching to the pixies!

'What did I tell you?' he shouted. 'Didn't I say that too much kindness was foolishness? Well, so it is! You melted that poor wretched snowman till he quite disappeared! He didn't walk away – he melted down to nothing! Ho, ho, ho! What do you think of that?'

Poor shivering snowman! Well – he had to melt some time, hadn't he?

3

Bubbly's Trick

Bubbly was a water-pixie. He lived in the little stream that ran through Buttercup Meadow, not far from the Wizard Twisty's cottage. Bubbly was a mischievous, naughty, tricky little pixie, always having a joke, always playing a prank.

'One day you will get into trouble!' said his brother Trickles. 'It's all very well to play tricks on me, Bubbly, or on the other water-pixies – but just be careful not to try your little games on the Wizard, or a passing witch!'

'Ooh! That's a fine idea!' said Bubbly at once. 'I'd love to trick old Twisty Wizard. Now let me think!'

'Don't be so silly!' said Trickles, and swam off in disgust.

Bubbly's Trick

Bubbly sat on a stone under the water and tickled a green frog, and thought and thought. He couldn't think of any trick to play on the Twisty Wizard, so he thought he would go up to the cottage where he lived, and see if any joke came into his head there. He swam to the edge of the stream, clambered out among the sweet-smelling water-mint, and ran through the buttercups and daisies to the wizard's crooked little cottage.

He peeped in at the window. The wizard was stirring a spell in a big dish by the window. He didn't see Bubbly's cheeky face peeping in. The water-pixie chuckled and rubbed his hands. He had thought of a fine trick! He would go and buy some sherbet at the sweet-shop – and when the wizard wasn't looking he would pop it into the bowl of magic – and it would all fizzle up and give old Twisty such a shock!

Off went Bubbly, and bought a penny-worth of white sherbet at the sweet-shop, in a paper bag. He stole

back to the cottage and peeped in. The wizard had finished stirring his bowl of magic, and was doing something to the fire at the other end of the room. Now was Bubbly's chance!

In a trice he put his hand in at the window, shook out the powder from the paper bag, and then waited to see what would happen.

The powder fell into the bowl of magic, where strange spells were stirring. As soon as the sherbet touched the magic liquid, there came a great sizzling noise and all the stuff in the bowl rose up like a snowdrift! It frothed over the edges of the bowl on to the table, and Bubbly grinned to see such a sight.

The Twisty Wizard turned round when he heard the sizzling noise. He stared at the frothing bowl in the greatest astonishment. Then he rushed to it, shouting: 'The spell has gone wrong! Jumping broomsticks, the spell has gone wrong!'

He took up the bowl and threw all the magic in it straight out of the window! And, as you know, Bubbly was just outside - so it all went over him in a trice!

He fell down in a fright, soaked through - and oh my, whatever do you think? When he got up, he had turned bright blue! He looked down at himself in horror and fear - a bright blue pixie! Whatever would everyone say to him!

'Oh, oh, oh!' wailed Bubbly, quite forgetting he was just outside the

Bubbly's Trick

window. The wizard heard him howling, and at once popped his head out. When he saw Bubbly there, he growled like an angry dog, stretched out his hand and grabbed hold of the frightened

pixie. In a moment he was standing in the kitchen before the furious wizard.

'Did you put anything into my bowl of magic?' roared Twisty.

'Yes,' sobbed Bubbly. 'I put in some sherbet, and it made it all fizzle up.'

41

'You wicked, mischievous, interfering, meddling creature!' cried the angry wizard. 'That spell took me four months to make – and now I have thrown it out of the window!'

'It's made me all blue,' sobbed Bubbly.

'Of course it has!' said Twisty. 'It was a spell to make blue lightning – so it turned you blue as quick as lightning! What's your name?'

'B-B-Bubbly!' said the pixie.

'Oho! I've heard of you before!' said Twisty. 'You're the pixie that makes himself a nuisance to everybody by playing stupid tricks. All right – this is the last trick you play! I shall send you to the Gobble-up Dragon to be eaten!'

Now Bubbly was indeed frightened. He tried hard to think of some way of escape. How could he outwit the wizard? He must think hard!

'Yes!' he said at last. 'Send me to Gobble-up! I don't care what you do with me so long as you don't drown me!'

'Oh! So you don't mind going to Gobble-up!' said Twisty. 'Well, if it's no punishment, I won't send you there. I'll pop you into my big saucepan, turn you into a goose, and have you for dinner!'

'Yes, do, do that!' said Bubbly. 'But please, I do beg of you, don't drown me!'

'Oh, so you like being turned into a goose, do you,' said Twisty. 'Well, I'll

think of something else. I'll sit you on a
broomstick that will take you to the
Greeneye Witch. You can be her
servant for a hundred years!'

'That would be nice,' said Bubbly.
'Yes, do, do that, Twisty Wizard.
Anything, if only you won't drown me!'

'What! You'd like to go to the
Greeneye Witch,' said the wizard, in
surprise. 'Well, I certainly won't send
you there! I will turn you into a green
frog and give you to my pet duck!'

45

'Oh, do!' said Bubbly. 'I'd like that –
but please – please don't drown me!'

'Well – I think I *will* drown you,
seeing that you are so scared of that!'
said the wizard, spitefully. He caught
hold of Bubbly, and dragged him out of
the cottage and down to the stream.
Then he threw him SPLASH into the
water, and stood by to watch what

happened, rubbing his hands in glee to
think what a fearful punishment he
had given the pixie.

But Bubbly swam to the other side at
once in delight. Then he popped out his

cheeky head, now a bright blue, and sang out: 'I'm so pleased to be home, Twisty, I'm so pleased to be home! Many, many thanks to you!'

Then he swam off to tell his brother all about it. The bright blue gradually wore off – but he still has blue ears – so if you meet him you are sure to know him – mischievous, cheeky little Bubbly!

4

The Lost Hum

In the nursery cupboard there was a big humming-top. The toys loved it very much, for often when it spun round and round, and hummed loudly, it would let some of the smaller toys sit on it and hold tightly to the handle. Then they had a fine ride, as you can imagine.

But one day the humming top didn't hum! It spun round and round, but not a single hum came out of it. It was most strange.

'What has happened?' wondered the toys.

'I think it must be because Eileen sat on the top yesterday, and bent it,' said the monkey. 'It must have spoilt the hum. What a pity!'

The top was sad. What was the use of being a humming-top if you couldn't hum? It sat and moped in the corner, and wouldn't even spin itself to give

the small dolls and the Noah's ark animals a ride.

'We must get back your hum some-how,' said the sailor doll. So one by one the toys tried to mend the hum. They pulled the handle straight. They rubbed up the silver sides. They blew in the

holes – but it wasn't a bit of good. No hum came from the top at all.

'We will go to the bees and ask them if they will give us a hum for you,' said the sailor doll at last. 'They hum loudly, and it would be lovely if we could get a good bee-hum for you! We will go tonight!'

So that night the monkey and the sailor doll climbed down the apple-tree that grew outside the nursery window, and went to the bee-hive. The bees were all inside, asleep. Not a hum was to be heard. The monkey knocked on the hive.

'Zzzzz!' said a sleepy bee at the door and he peeped out. 'What do you want?'

'Could you spare a good hum for the

top in the nursery?' asked the monkey, politely.

'Zzzz! What will you give us if we do?' asked the bee.

'What do you want?' said the doll.

'There is nothing we want,' said the bee. 'But there's something we don't want!'

'What is that?' asked the doll, puzzled.

'Zzzzzz! Well, we don't want the blue tit to come and eat us as we go in and out of our hive,' said the bee. 'He flies down here and waits for us. Go and tell him not to do this, and get his promise – and we will give you a good hum for the top.'

So off to the blue tit's roosting-place went the monkey and the sailor doll. They climbed up the pear-tree, where the tit slept in a cosy hole, and rapped on the bark. The tit hissed and asked what they wanted.

'Will you promise not to go and eat the bees as they come in and out of the hive?' asked the monkey. 'We want a new hum for our top in the nursery and

they will give us one if you will promise not to eat them any more.'

'Well, what will you give me if I promise?' asked the tit, sleepily. 'I must have some food, mustn't I?'

'Well, what other food do you like?' asked the sailor doll.

'I love nuts,' said the tit. 'But no one has put out any nuts for me this year.'

'We will go and ask the squirrel for some nuts for you,' said the toys. So down they climbed and went to look for the frisky squirrel. They knew he lived in a tree-hole too – one much bigger

53

than the tiny one the tit slept in. They soon found the oak tree that the squirrel liked, and once more up they climbed. The squirrel was sound asleep and most astonished to see them.

'Nuts!' he said. 'Fancy coming and asking me for nuts at this time of night! You must be mad! What do you want them for?'

'To give to the tit,' said the doll. 'You see, if we take him some nuts, he says he will promise not to eat the bees, and then they will give us a hum for our big top in the nursery.'

'Well, I'll find you some nuts if you like,' said the squirrel, yawning, 'but you must do something for me if I get up now and hunt for them.'

'What would you like?' said the toys.

'I always hide my nuts in different places in the autumn,' said the squirrel. 'But when I wake up on a warm day, do you suppose I can remember where I have put them? No, I never can! Well, if you could get a notebook and put down in it all my hiding-places, and read them to me when I wake up on warm

days, that would be such a help. If you'll do that, I'll get you the nuts you want for the tit – and what is more, I'll get the kernel out for you, because I know the tit can't, with his little beak!'

The Lost Hum

'Oh, thank you!' said the toys joyfully. The sailor doll put his hand into his pocket and pulled out a very small notebook and tiny pencil. He was very proud of these and had never used them before. He licked the pencil and opened the book.

'Now, I'm ready!' he said to the squirrel. 'Tell me what to put down.'

'There are nuts in the hole under the roots of this tree,' said the squirrel, thinking. 'Have you got that down? And there are some in the ditch by that old boot. And I put some more behind

that thick ivy on the old wall. And the last lot I put in my own hole here. That's all.'

The doll wrote down all the hiding-places in his neat, small writing. Then he shut the book and put it into his pocket. 'Come to the nursery window whenever you wake up on warm winter days,' he said, 'and I will read you all your hiding-places. Then you will be able to eat your nuts whenever you like!'

'Thank you,' said the squirrel. He groped down in his hole and brought up four fine hazel nuts. He gnawed

them with his strong teeth, and made a hole in each one, so that the nut inside showed through. Then he gave the four gnawed shells to the doll.

'There you are!' he said. 'The tit can peck out the nut easily now.'

'Thank you,' said the toys, gratefully, and went to the tit's tree. He was delighted with the nuts, and began to peck the kernel of one at once.

'Will you give us your promise not to eat the bees now?' asked the monkey. The tit nodded his blue head.

'I promise!' he said. So off went the toys to the bee-hive and told the bees the good news. Two or three of them were waiting for the toys at the hive entrance. They were delighted to know that the tit would no longer come to eat them as they went in and out of the hive.

'Zzzzz!' they said. 'Good! Now, toys, take this little pinch of yellow powder, and put it into the holes round the sides of the top. Spin the top well immediately afterwards, and you will find that it hums as loudly as a hive of bees!'

The toys thanked the bees and hurried off once more. They climbed up the apple-tree and slid down to the floor. They ran to the top and emptied the fine yellow powder into all the holes.

Then, amid great excitement – for all the toys had come out of the cupboard to watch – the monkey spun the big top round and round.

'Zzzzzzzzzzzz!' hummed the top, so loudly that the monkey was afraid it would wake everyone up! He stopped the top in a hurry, and all the toys laughed in delight. The top had got a beautiful hum – much better than before! What fun! Now, it would be happy again, and not lie in a corner and mope.

The squirrel hasn't been to ask where his nuts are yet – but one winter's morning, when the sun is shining brightly he'll peep in at the toys – and then the sailor doll will pull out his notebook and tell him all those hiding-places! I wish I could hear him telling the squirrel, don't you?

5

The Flying Kite

The kite was very angry. It was a windy day, and Eric had taken it up to the hill to fly it. He hadn't very much string, so the kite couldn't fly very high. It tugged and it tugged, but Eric held it firmly.

'Let me fly higher, let me fly higher!' sang the kite. 'The wind is strong, I want to go. Let me fly up, up, up!'

But Eric held on even more tightly, and that made the kite crosser still! It gave an enormous tug – and broke the string! Ah, then it was free, and it went sailing up and up into the air, as high as could be, simply delighted. Eric was very sad. He had lost his beautiful yellow kite. He went home crying.

But the kite didn't care. 'I don't belong to anyone now!' it sang. 'I'm all alone! I can go where I wish! I shall fly to the moon!'

But suddenly the wind dropped – and so did the kite! It fell down, down, down to earth, and, dear me, it went splash into a small pond, frightening all the ducks and sending them off in a hurry.

'Oh!' said the kite, feeling cold and wet. 'I am sinking! I want to fly! Eric, where are you? Come and save me!'

But Eric was far away. The kite got wetter and wetter. Then a dog came by and saw it in the pond. It splashed in and got hold of it. It brought it to the

bank in its mouth, and bit two big holes in it. Then it left it there on the bank and ran off.

The wind dried the kite and so did the sun. It lay there, feeling very sorry for itself, with two holes in its pretty yellow canvas. Then suddenly it felt the wind lifting it again and off it went, high in the air, its tail swinging below it.

'I'm off, I'm off!' cried the kite. 'Where shall I go? To the moon. Yes, to the moon.'

But soon it dipped down again, and down and down – and oh dear, what a dreadful thing, it fell into a bonfire! The wind lifted it off again – but its tail was burnt right off and went up in smoke.

'Now I've no tail!' wept the kite. 'How shall I fly without a tail?'

It lay there until night came and then the wind found it again and once more whipped it up into the air. It flew very high, even without a tail, but it kept turning upside down and round and round, for it now had no tail to steady it. It felt very giddy, and didn't like it at all.

'Why did I fly away from Eric?' thought the kite, sadly. 'Better to be safe on the end of a string, than never to know what is going to happen to me!'

The wind dropped towards dawn – and down went the kite once more to

The Flying Kite

earth. This time it dropped into a field where two donkeys slept. When the sun rose and lighted up the field one of the donkeys awoke and saw the big yellow kite not far off. It wondered what it could be and walked up to it. 'Perhaps it is good to eat,' thought the donkey.

He began to nibble round the edge, and the kite was full of fear.

'Don't eat me!' it cried, but the donkey didn't hear. It went on nibbling and soon the other donkey came and nibbled too.

Goodness knows what would have happened to the kite if the farmer's little boy hadn't come running into the field then, and seen the kite. He shooed the donkeys away and picked up the kite.

'Oh!' he cried joyfully. 'It's a fine yellow kite! My! Wouldn't it fly beautifully if I made it a tail and mended these holes and these ragged bits where the donkeys have nibbled!'

He took the kite home. His mother mended all the holes, and his father made a tail of string and paper. It wasn't a very good tail – but quite good enough to help the kite to fly.

'It's windy to-day,' said the little boy. 'I'll take it up to the hill and fly it.'

So off he went. He had the tiniest ball of string, all his mother could give him, and the kite couldn't get higher than the telegraph wires – but do you suppose it minded? Not a bit of it! It was as pleased as could be, and didn't tug at all, except just a little when the wind blew hard.

'How lovely to be held safely on a string!' thought the kite, joyfully. 'What fun to fly like this! I shall never be discontented again. I will give pleasure to this little boy, instead of trying to find pleasure for myself. Then I shall be happy!'

The farmer's little boy still flies the old yellow kite and they are both as happy as can be!

6

Three Bad Brownies

There were once three brownies called Snip, Snap and Snorum. They lived a wandering life, and earned what money they could by doing odd jobs for people.

Now one day they came to the castle of Witch Thingumebob. She was a very powerful witch, and was always making the most surprising and extra-

ordinary spells. She had a faithful
servant and helper, a large black cat
with golden eyes and a kink in his long
tail. Cinders was his name, and he
used to get his mistress anything she
wanted for her spells.

But one evening she asked him to get
something and he shook his head. 'No,
madam,' he said. 'I cannot get those.'
The witch wanted to make a spell
that would turn people into spiteful

creatures – she thought she would use it on the fairies, who were always happy together, and kind. Oho! That would make a disturbance in Fairyland, to have the fairies fighting and clawing each other like cats!

But to make this spell Thingumebob needed the pointed claws of twelve cats – and Cinders would not get them for her.

'No,' he said, each time she commanded him. 'I will not get those. I will

not rob my brothers and sisters and cousins of their weapons.'

So when Snip, Snap and Snorum turned up, she was pleased to see them, for she knew they would do anything to get a few pence.

'Can we do anything for you, Madam Thingumebob?' asked Snip, bowing.

'Yes,' said the witch. 'I want the claws of twelve cats. If you get me these, I will give you a gold piece each.'

'Very well,' said Snip, Snap and

73

Snorum, and went out of the castle in glee. A gold piece each! What riches!

'Now,' said Snorum, 'I know where we'll go! The Lord High Chamberlain of Fairyland lives near here, and he has a great many cats for he is very fond of them. We'll go and snip off the claws of twelve of them. We need not hurt the cats – it will be just like cutting

their nails – and it doesn't hurt us to cut ours, does it!'

They made their way to the Chamberlain's beautiful castle, set high up on a hill. They peeped in at the garden and saw many lovely cats sitting about, or sleeping. Nearby was a great dish of cream. In a trice Snap was over the wall and had emptied a sleepy spell into the cream. The cats thought he was putting something tasty in their dish, and they ran up to see. A good many of them licked the cream, and no sooner had they done that than they lay down and fell fast asleep!

'Now!' said Snap, and he took out his scissors. 'Where's the bag to put the claws in, Snip? Snorum, you keep a lookout in case anyone comes!'

In five minutes Snap had neatly cut the tips of twelve cats' claws, and had

popped them into the bag that Snip held open for him. The little curved nails slipped inside. Snip, Snap and Snorum, their job finished, climbed over the wall again – but dear me, just as they were dropping down on the other side, a stern voice cried out to them: 'What are you doing?'

And there was the Lord High Chamberlain himself, standing nearby, on his way to his garden gate!

'N-n-n-n-nothing!' stammered Snap.

'What have you in your sack?' demanded the Chamberlain.

'N-n-n-n-nothing!' stuttered Snip.

'Show me!' said the Chamberlain.

'N-n-n-no!' shouted Snorum, and the three took to their heels and fled through the wood that surrounded the castle.

'Cats! After them!' shouted the Chamberlain – and in a moment all the cats on the other side of the wall, even those that had been asleep, swarmed up and dropped down from the wall, racing after the three wicked brownies. The Chamberlain raced with them.

Snip, Snap and Snorum looked behind them in despair. They would never be able to reach the witch's castle in time. Never! They raced on and on, and soon they were quite lost in the wood. Behind them came all the cats,

Three Bad Brownies

and the shouting Chamberlain.

'I can't go any farther,' gasped Snip, sitting down under a bush. 'I can't, I can't!'

The others crawled under the bush, too. Snip opened the sack, took out all the cats' claws and flung them quickly into the bush above them.

'Grow! Grow!' he commanded – and all the little curved claws fastened themselves to the stems – and grew there.

Up came the Chamberlain and his cats and very soon the three brownies were discovered and dragged out. Their sack was opened – and it was empty!

'They cut off the claws of twelve of us!' mewed one of the cats.

'Where are the claws?' demanded the Chamberlain angrily. But the brownies would not tell him. He crawled under the bush, thinking that perhaps they had hidden the claws there. And the big prickles on the bush caught hold of him and scratched him. He realised what had happened! The claws had

been thrown into the bush and had grown on the stems!

'Get out of Fairyland!' he commanded the frightened brownies. 'And if ever I hear of any tricks again, I'll set my cats on you, and let you feel what their claws are like when they have grown again! Now go quickly.'

The brownies went – they scuttled through the trees like rabbits and didn't stop until they had reached the gates of Fairyland and gone through. They were so afraid of those cats – and I dare say it won't surprise you to know that whenever they see a cat now they turn tail and run off in fright!

The Chamberlain went home with his cats, whose claws soon grew again. And what about the bush on whose stems the little curved claws grew?

Well, you can see it still. It is the blackberry bush, so prickly and scratchy! Look at the stems, and you will see the little curved claws of the cats. It is no wonder that the brambles are so scratchy, is it!

7

The Bad-Tempered Doll

Emmeline was a very bad-tempered doll. She flew into a rage over everything, and smacked the other toys and pinched them and kicked them. Goodness, what a little monkey she was!

Now, one day, Sally, the little girl that Emmeline belonged to, planned a treat for all her toys.

'We will go and have a picnic in the woods tomorrow,' she said. 'I will take you all in the big doll's pram. I can pack you there very comfortably. You shall go, Emmeline, and you Clock-work clown, and you, Monkey, and you, Teddy-bear, and you, Donald Duck, and you, Peter Rabbit. It will be a bit of a squash in the pram, but never mind. We shall have a lovely time when we get there.'

Now, that night, when the toys were talking about the treat they were going to have, Emmeline, the bad-tempered doll, was very angry.

'To think that I've got to ride all squashed up with you in my pram!' she

shouted to the toys. 'What does Sally want to take you all for? Why doesn't she just take me alone, in my pram? Oh, won't I give you a bad time to-

morrow, Clown; I shall take your key
out and throw it into the road, where it
will be lost for ever and ever.'

'You mustn't do that,' said the clown
in alarm.

'Monkey, I shall pinch you till you
are even blacker than you are now,'
said Emmeline to the monkey. 'And,
Teddy-bear, I'll pull your ears off. As
for you, Donald Duck, I'll press your
quack till it breaks – and I'll pull Peter
Rabbit's whiskers out. Sally won't
notice anything – I'll have a lovely
time with you all, in my pram to-
morrow. You just wait.'

'You're a very bad-tempered doll,'

said the clock-work clown. 'And you'd better be careful, or you'll be sorry.'

'I'm never sorry,' said the doll, and she made an ugly face.

Now, the toys were very upset to hear all this. They knew perfectly well that Emmeline would do all she said. They would be covered up with the pram-cover and Sally wouldn't see anything at all.

'I'm not going to have my key thrown out into the road,' said the clown crossly.

'And I'm not going to be pinched till I'm blacker than I am now,' said Monkey.

'And I *won't* have my ears pulled off,'

said the bear fiercely. 'They're very useful to me.'

'And I won't have my quack spoilt,' said Donald Duck.

'And I won't have my whiskers pulled out,' said Peter Rabbit, who was proud of his fine grey whiskers, and curled them up nicely once a week.

'But what are we to DO?' said the clown.

'Anybody got any good ideas?' asked panda.

Nobody had.

'I do wish Emmeline would have a bad cold and have to stay in bed,' said Teddy-bear.

'She's never had a cold in her life,' said Donald Duck. 'She doesn't even know what it is to sneeze.'

'Huh! I could soon make her do that with a shake of the pepper-pot,' said the clown. 'A sniff of pepper would make anyone sneeze.'

Donald Duck suddenly had the finest idea of his life. 'I say, toys,' he said in a whisper, in case Emmeline should hear him. 'I say! What about making her sneeze – and sneeze – *and* sneeze! Then Sally will think she has a cold and make her stay in bed for the day – and we shall be able to have our treat without her!'

'Donald Duck, I always thought you were a stupid fellow till now,' said Teddy-bear in great excitement, 'but you are not – you are the cleverest of us all! The very thing! Pepper – to make her sneeze – and sneeze – *and* sneeze! What a joke!'

'How shall we do it?' asked Peter Rabbit, his nose woffling in excitement.

'Let me think,' said the clown, who was really the best at thinking when a lot of it had to be done. 'Yes – I know. I'll hide behind Emmeline's cot early this morning – with the pepper-pot out of the nursery cupboard. And I'll shake the pepper out as soon as I see Sally coming in, and make Emmeline sneeze her head off!'

So that night the clown got the pepper-pot out of the cupboard and crept behind the cot where Emmeline slept. There he waited till the morning – and as soon as he saw Sally coming in, he quickly shook some pepper out into the air. It flew to Emmeline's nose.

'A-tish-oo!' said Emmeline at once.

Sally heard her and looked anxiously at her doll.

'Oh dear, Emmeline, I hope you haven't got a cold!' she said.

'No, of course I–a-TISH-oo!' said Emmeline.

'Emmeline, you *have* got a cold!' cried Sally. 'Oh dear, I wonder how you got it!'

90

The Bad-Tempered Doll

'I *haven't* got a-TISH-OO!' sneezed Emmeline, getting crosser and crosser. 'A-tish-oo! A-tish-oo!'

The clown was shaking the pepper-pot well. In fact he shook it so well that he suddenly felt as if he were going to sneeze himself. That would never do! He pressed his nose hard and stopped the sneeze.

'Emmeline, have you a headache too?' asked Sally. 'I don't think I can let you go with me to the woods today.'

'Oh, I want to go, I want to – a-TISH-oo!' said Emmeline. 'Oh, bother this

sneezing! I can't stop! A-tish-oo!'

'Do you feel very ill, Emmeline?' asked Sally.

'A-tish-oo!' said Emmeline.

'Did you feel cold when you were out yesterday?' asked Sally, feeling her doll's hands to see if they were hot.

'A-tish-oo!' said Emmeline.

'Well, darling Emmeline, you simply can't come to the woods for a picnic to-day,' said Sally. 'You must have got a dreadful cold! You must stay in bed and I will take the others.'

'Boo-hoo – a-tish-oo! boo-hoo – a-tish-

oo!' wept and sneezed Emmeline.

'You do sound funny,' said Sally. 'Now lie still and be a good doll. I'm going to get the others ready.'

In twenty minutes Donald Duck, Clockwork Clown, Monkey, Bear, and Peter Rabbit were all tucked into the doll's pram. How they giggled and

chuckled when they heard poor Emmeline in her cot sneezing and crying loudly.

'It serves you right!' called Teddy-

The Bad-Tempered Doll

bear, when Sally had gone to get the pram-cover. 'It serves you right!'

'It doesn't serve me – a-tish-oo!' cried Emmeline. 'A-tish-oo! Oh, why am I sneezing? I haven't got a cold. I know I haven't!'

The toys went off in the pram with Sally and had a perfectly lovely picnic in the woods. You should have seen them! And when they got home they found that Emmeline had quite stopped sneezing and was feeling very sad and lonely.

'Why, Emmeline, I don't believe you've got a cold after all!' said Sally in surprise. 'I do wonder why you sneezed such a lot this morning!'

'Ask the pepper-pot!' said the clown in a loud whisper – and Sally wondered why all the toys suddenly began to giggle!

8

The Shepherd Boy & the Goblin

There was once a shepherd boy who lived out on the hills, watching his sheep. With him was his dog, Lassie, a wise and loving animal, ready to do anything in the world for her little master.

There were goblins on the hillside. Dick, the shepherd boy, had often seen them, and had kept well out of their way, for he knew them to be ill-natured creatures, and ready to catch him and make him their servant if they only could!

One night, Dick saw a goblin coming along quietly with an empty sack over his back. He did not see the shepherd boy, who was behind a bush with his dog. Lassie was about to growl, but Dick laid his hand on her and she lay silent.

Dick peered round the bush in the moonlight. To his enormous surprise he saw the goblin go to a stone that lay close to the hillside and twist it round. An entrance to a cave showed up, big and black.

'So that's where the goblins go to get their treasure!' thought Dick. 'Oho! I may pay that cave a visit myself, if I have a chance!'

He watched till the goblin came out again, this time with a *full* sack on his shoulder. The little creature staggered down the hill, muttering to himself, and as he went something rolled out of the sack.

When the goblin had gone, Dick picked up what had rolled from the sack. It was a gleaming diamond! The boy whistled in surprise. Riches in the hill! Riches to make his mother and father, and all his sisters and brothers happy, well-fed and well-shod! Aha! He would take a sack himself and go to fill it that very morning.

He called his father to look after the sheep, and whistled to his dog, Lassie, to come with him. Then, a sack over his shoulder, and his dog by his side, the

boy went to the big stone in the hillside.

He twisted it as he had seen the goblin do. It swung round – and there lay the black, cold cave! Dick stepped inside and the dog came too. He went in for a good way – and then stopped in wonder! All round the cave-wall glisten-ed brilliant stones, some green, some red, some white, some blue!

'I shall be richer than any man in the world!' thought the boy. He began to fill his sack full. In went the precious stones, one on top of another till the sack was almost too heavy to lift. When it would hold not one more stone Dick began to lift it on to his shoulder.

And then a harsh voice spoke in the darkness of the cave.

'You have filled your sack well, shepherd boy! Can you not get one more thing into it?'

A lantern shone, and a goblin crept out of the darkness. Then came another goblin – and another – and another. The boy was surrounded, and his heart beat fast as he saw so many of the ugly little creatures coming near to him.

Lassie growled, but Dick stopped her.

He was afraid that the goblins might turn her into a rock or a clod of earth if she offended them.

'Ho!' said the first goblin, peering into the sack. 'A good haul! How dare you come and rob us of our jewels?'

'They are not yours,' said Dick. 'They belong to anyone who finds them. This hill does not belong to you!'

'Oh, yes, it does!' said the goblin. 'It has been ours for nine-hundred years! See, brothers! See how many of our precious stones he meant to steal!'

'It is a wonder he could lift the sack!' said another, angrily.

'He could not get one more stone in!' said a third. 'It is full to the brim! Anything else would roll out!'

'How shall we punish him?' asked the first goblin.

'He shall serve us for one-hundred years and a day!' shouted all the goblins.

'That I will not!' said Dick stoutly. 'You have no right to keep me here. I will not take your jewels, if you think

them yours. I will leave them here in the sack. Now let me go, or it will be the worse for you.'

'And who do you think will find you here?' said the first goblin, mockingly. 'No one knows this cave save ourselves. No, my boy – you shall be our servant. You shall fetch and carry, cook and sweep. How you will long to see the sun - for never again will you step outside this hill!'

'Do not keep me here,' said Dick. 'Let me go. I must see to my sheep. I am sorry I took your jewels. I will keep the secret of your cave to myself. No one shall ever know it.'

'Shall we let him go, brothers?' said the first goblin, with a wicked grin.

'Yes - on one condition!' shouted another goblin. 'If he - or his dog—can put another thing into that full sack, we will let them go!'

'Ho, ho!' roared the goblins, knowing quite well that the sack was already full to the brim. 'Yes! Now, boy, try!' But try as he would, Dick could not get anything else into that sack! Stones rolled out - earth would not stay - nothing else could be put there, for the sack was already quite full.

The dog was lying watching, her big brown eyes wise and thoughtful. When her master had finished trying, and

was sitting in despair on the cave floor, the dog stood up and went to the sack.

'And now the dog is going to try!' shouted the mischievous goblins, enjoying their cruel joke. 'Come, dog – if *you* can put anything more into the sack, you and your master shall go free!'

'Woof!' said Lassie – and she straightway bit a large hole in the sack. Then she turned to Dick, who had sprung to his feet in delight.

'She has put something in the sack that wasn't there before!' he cried. 'She has put a hole in it! See! *Now* what do you say, goblins? Set us free!'

The goblins frowned and grumbled and shook their fists at Lassie – but it was no use, they must keep their word and set the boy and the dog free. Sullenly, they stood aside to let them pass, and the two ran up the dark cave and out into the golden sunshine.

'Lassie, Lassie, you clever dog!' cried Dick, hugging the delighted animal, who licked him again and again. 'You are wiser than I am! What should I have done without you!'

He ran to tell his father his adventure – and suddenly he remembered the diamond he had found the night before. He took it from his pocket and showed it to his father.

'We will sell it,' said the man, overjoyed. 'It will buy us many good things.'

It did – and what do you suppose was the very first thing it bought? A new collar for Lassie with her name on it in gold!

'You deserve it!' cried Dick, as he put it on. And she certainly did.

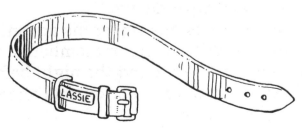

9

The Mischievous Tunnel

Jimmy had a railway train that ran by clockwork on toy railway-lines. He had a little station too, with porters and passengers standing on it. He had a fine signal that went up and down – and he had a tunnel for the train to go under.

But that tunnel was too mischievous for anything! It always managed to set itself just a bit crooked when the train came rushing through – and, of course, the engine knocked into it, ran off the lines, and fell over. Then Jimmy would shout loudly:

'An accident! An accident!'

The tunnel thought this was great fun. It didn't matter how carefully Jimmy set the tunnel over the lines, it always managed to make itself crooked when the train came running by. And always there was an accident.

At first Jimmy and Jane, his sister, thought this was rather fun. But when it happened every time they got tired of it. 'I wish the train would run round and round properly until the clockwork runs down,' said Jimmy. 'It always falls off by the tunnel.'

'Well, it shouldn't,' said Jane, looking through the tunnel. 'The tunnel doesn't touch the lines, Jimmy. It's supposed to be quite wide enough for the train to run through. I think it's a mischievous

111

tunnel. Look – I've set it so that the train can run right through without touching at all.'

'All right,' said Jimmy. 'I'll put lots of passengers on the train, Jane, and give them a good trip. And I'll put some toy cows into the cow-trucks too. The guard can go in the guard's van. My, it's a full train. It mustn't have an accident this time!'

Well, when the tunnel heard what a lot of passengers were going to be on the train, it felt more mischievous than ever. It would certainly upset the train if it could – and then what a lot of people would fall out!

So once again it set itself just a bit crooked so that it touched the line.

Jimmy wound up the engine. The signal looked at the crooked tunnel and spoke to it.

'Tunnel! I can see you've put yourself crooked. Now don't play tricks this time. You know quite well that Jimmy

113

and Jane are tired of them. Don't upset the train.'

'I shall do as I like,' said the tunnel, and set itself more crooked than ever.

Jimmy set the engine down on the line. He hooked the coal-truck on to it. Behind were all the carriages, the cow-trucks, and the guard's van.

It was a fine long train, but the engine was strong and could quite well pull them all.

Jimmy waved his green flag. The signal worked. Jane whistled. The train was off.

Round the lines it sped, as fast as it could, and behind it ran all the trucks as happy as could be, with the dolls jerking up and down in them, and the cows looking out of their trucks too.

114

The engine reached the tunnel. Its key
caught against it. It ran off the lines.
The carriages all fell over. Out tumbled
the dolls and the cows. Another accident
– and a bad one this time!

'Oh dear! This little doll has broken her arm!' said Jane. 'And this cow has broken off her tail. Bother that horrid tunnel. We won't use it for a tunnel any more!'

Jane picked up the tunnel and put it away from the lines.

'But what else can you use a tunnel for?' Jimmy asked.

'I'll soon show you!' said Jane, and she went to the doll's chest. She took out a little mattress, a pillow, a bolster, two sheets, and two blankets. She turned the tunnel upside down, and neatly arranged all the bedclothes inside.

'It shall be a cradle for my baby doll!' she said. 'I haven't a bed small enough for her – and the tunnel will do nicely. If it can't behave like a proper tunnel, it shall behave like a cradle!'

Well, you should have heard the signal and the porters, the passengers and the engine driver laugh when they saw what was happening to the tunnel. A baby doll's cradle! Well, well, well!

116

As for tunnel, it was in a great rage; but it couldn't turn itself the right way up – so there it is still, a nice little cradle for the baby doll. And doesn't it wish it was a proper tunnel again, watching the railway train rush round and round and round! Maybe if Jimmy ever gives it another chance it will really try to behave itself.

10

Funny Little Shorty

Bobby brought a new toy home with him one night. He put it in the toy cupboard.

'There you are, little cat,' he said. 'Make friends with all my other toys!'

He shut the cupboard door and went off to bed. The toys stared at the new toy in silence. What would he be like?

'Hello!' said the new toy. 'Let's go out and have a run round the playroom, shall we? I'd like to see my new home.'

They all went out into the big playroom. It was a nice place, with rugs over the floor. 'Ha, good!' said the new toy, and he gave a little run and then slid all the way along the slippery floor on his four black legs.

'You don't do things like that until we know you better,' said Rosebud, the big doll.

'Oh dear – sorry!' said the new toy, and he sat down on the nearby rug. 'How long will it take for you to know me better? There's not much to know about me, really.'

'What are you?' asked the pink rabbit.

119

'Well – can't you see? I'm a cat, of course,' said the new toy.

'You're not,' said the toy dog at once. 'You haven't got a tail. All cats have tails.'

'Not the kind of cat I am,' said the cat. 'I'm a toy cat from the Isle of Man – and Manx cats don't have long tails.'

'I don't believe you,' said the toy monkey, swinging his lovely long tail. 'You're just saying that to make us think it's all right for you not to have a tail. You must have lost your tail somewhere. Don't tell stories!'

'I am *not*,' said the little Manx cat, crossly. 'I never tell stories. I'm telling you the truth. I'm a little Manx cat, and Manx cats don't have tails – or only just a stump, like mine. Do believe me.'

But they didn't. They only laughed at the little toy cat. 'We shall call you Shorty, because your tail is so very, very short that you almost haven't got one,' said the monkey. 'You look silly, Shorty. You ought to try and get a tail from somewhere. One like mine!'

120

'I don't want a tail,' said Shorty. 'I should feel strange with one. I tell you I'm the kind of cat that doesn't have one. So I don't want one. Is there a teddy bear here? Yes, I can see him. Well, he hasn't got a tail either – but you don't laugh at him.'

'No, because he's not supposed to have one, so he looks all right without one," said the toy dog, wagging his tail to show how strong it was. 'You just look silly without one. All cats have tails.'

Shorty gave up. 'All right,' he said. 'Have it your own way. But let me tell you this – I think you're all rather silly and very unkind. I do think you might be more friendly to a new toy.'

But the toys weren't nice to Shorty. They turned away from him and wouldn't show him round the playroom.

They didn't talk to him much either, and they never asked him to join in their games. He was very sad about it.

'I can't help not having a tail,' he thought. 'What difference does a tail make? I wish I lived in the Isle of Man where it's strange for a cat to have a tail. Oh well – I must just make the best of things.'

So Shorty didn't quarrel or grumble. He was always cheerful and smiling and willing to do anything for anyone. He was even glad to wind up the clockwork mouse when the others got tired of it.

'It's a pity you haven't a long, long tail like mine, Shorty,' the mouse said each time the toy cat wound him up. 'You do look odd, you know.'

'Rubbish!' said Shorty, cheerfully. 'There you are – your key won't turn any more, so you are fully wound up. Run along.'

Now one day a really dreadful thing happened. A little girl came to tea with Bobby, and they quarrelled. Bobby wouldn't let her take his mother's scissors from her workbasket and use them to cut pictures out of his books.

'No, Jennifer,' he said. 'For one thing I'm not allowed to have those scissors, and nor are you. And for another thing I won't let you spoil my books. You spoil your own, I know – but I like my books.'

Jennifer was angry. She was a spoilt, loud-voiced little girl, and she shouted at Bobby.

'You're a meanie, that's what you are! A meanie! I don't like you. I'll break your train!'

'No, you won't,' said Bobby, and he took his train and went into the bedroom. He locked it up in a drawer and came back. But while he had gone Jennifer had run to the workbasket and taken the scissors. Her mean little eyes gleamed. She would pay Bobby back for doing that!

'Go and see what the time is,' she said to Bobby. 'I think it must be getting late.'

Bobby went down to the hall to look at the big grandfather clock there. He hoped it was getting late, then this horrid girl would go.

Jennifer waited until he was out of

the room, then she ran to the toy cupboard and opened it. She pulled out the monkey, the toy dog, the clockwork mouse, the little kangaroo that could jump, and the lovely little horse with his long, long tail.

And what do you think she did? She cut off all their tails! Then she stuffed the toys back into the cupboard, and put the tails in her pocket. She heard

Bobby coming back and hurriedly put the scissors into her pocket too. The sharp end stuck into her and hurt her. She began to cry.

'What's the matter?' said Bobby. But Jennifer couldn't tell him, of course. She just said she wanted to go home, and off she went, wondering what Bobby would say when he saw his spoilt toys.

Bobby didn't see them that evening – but, oh dear, what an upset there was when the toys streamed out of the cupboard that night! How they cried.

Shorty was very sorry for them all, because he knew how much they thought of their tails. He tried to comfort them.

'Cheer up. Perhaps we can make other tails, just as nice as yours. Don't cry.'

'Don't be silly,' said the monkey. 'Where can we get new tails?'

'I can find you one,' said Shorty, and he pointed to where the curtain was looped back with a long silky cord. 'A

127

bit of that would look fine on you!'

'So it would,' said the monkey, wiping his eyes. In a trice Shorty had snipped a piece off the curtain loop and had given it to Rosebud to sew on to the monkey.

'Find me a tail, find me a tail!'begged the little clockwork mouse, running up to him.

'There's a very nice piece of black string in the string-box," said Shorty. 'It would make you a wonderful tail!'

And it did. You should have seen the clockwork mouse with his new black tail. It was even longer than his old one.

Shorty was very clever. He found an old furry collar belonging to Rosebud the doll. She said she didn't want it, so he carefully cut it up into two pieces, and made tails for the toy dog and the kangaroo. They were simply delighted.

'My new tail wags better than the old one,' said the toy dog, and he wagged it.

'What about me, please, Shorty?' neighed the little horse. 'My tail was so beautiful – it was made of hairs, you know.'

'Yes, I know it was,' said Shorty, thoughtfully. 'Now, let me see – what would be best for your tail? Oh, I know! What about taking some hairs from the old rug by the fireplace?'

So he pulled twenty hairs from the rug and neatly tied them together. Then Rosebud sewed on the new tail and the little horse swished it about in delight.

'You're very, very kind,' said the monkey, in rather a small voice.

'Yes, you are,' said all the toys.

'You've bothered about new tails for us,' said the toy dog, 'but you haven't even thought of one for yourself. We've teased you and teased you – and instead of being glad when we had no tails, like you, you were sorry and made some for us. Do, do make yourself a tail, too.'

'No, don't,' said Rosebud, suddenly. 'I like you without a tail, Shorty. I do really. You wouldn't be Shorty if you had a tail!'

'But wouldn't you all like me better with one?' said Shorty, surprised. 'I could make one, of course. I just didn't think of it for myself.'

'No, Shorty, no!' cried all the toys, and the little kangaroo came and hugged him. 'We like you as you are. It's funny – but you look nice without a

tail. Don't have one! You wouldn't be our nice old Shorty!'

Shorty beamed all over his whiskery face. 'All right,' he said. 'I won't have one. I don't want one, because I'm not supposed to wear a tail, anyway! Well – are we all going to be good friends now?'

Funny Little Shorty

'Yes – if you'll have us,' said the pink rabbit, looking rather ashamed of himself. 'And listen, Shorty, if anyone is ever unkind to you again, just go and pull his tail!'

'All right,' said Shorty, with a grin. 'But I shan't need to!'

And he didn't, of course. They were all good friends after that – but Bobby *is* puzzled about all the new tails!

11

Peter's Big Magnet

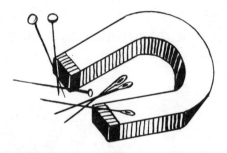

Peter had a big magnet. It was shaped like a horseshoe, and was painted red except just at the two ends, which were black. Peter thought his magnet must have some magic about it, for it would pick up needles as easily as anything, and would even draw his sister's little scissors to itself, and make them stick on to the two ends. He loved playing with it.

'Let me have your needles and scissors,' he would say to Eileen, his sister.

'I'll show your dolls and toys how to work magic!'

Then he would show Eileen and the toys how the needles would move to the magnet and how the scissors would hold on to it even when he held the magnet high in the air. The scissors would not let go – they couldn't! They stuck on the magnet as if they were glued there!

Then after a time Peter became tired of his big magnet and it was put into the toy cupboard with all the other things. The toys were rather afraid of it

134

at first, for they wondered if it would make them stick to it, as the scissors had done. But it didn't seem to do anything to them, and after a time they took no notice of it at all.

Now one day a small red goblin came into the nursery out of a mouse-hole in

the wall. The toys didn't like the look of him at all. He was a most unpleasant little creature, with green eyes, red hair, and a red suit. He grinned at the toys, pulled the baby doll's hair and pinched the panda.

'Don't!' said the panda. 'Go away!'

But the goblin laughed and wouldn't go away. He stole the sweets out of the toy sweet-shop, and then ran off when cock-crow came. He appeared the next

135

night and took some more sweets. The
toys were very angry for they were
afraid that Peter and Eileen might
think they had stolen the sweets.

Then the goblin began to steal other
things. He unpinned the brooch from
the fairy doll's frock and put it on
himself. The teddy-bear fought him for
that, but the goblin was such a quick
and nimble fellow that the bear couldn't
seem to hit him at all. The goblin
punched and pinched and soon the
poor bear had to give up the fight.

The next night the goblin stole the
blue tie that went round the panda's
neck. He dragged it off and tied it
round his own neck. It didn't suit him
very well, but he was pleased with it
and went into the doll's house to look at
himself in the mirror.

Then he took the shoes off the
talking-doll's feet and put them on his
own. His shoes were full of holes, and
he gave them to the doll instead of
hers. She cried bitterly, for she loved
her own pretty blue shoes. The toys
were furious with the unkind, wicked
little goblin, but he laughed at them,
and did just as he pleased!

Then one night he discovered Eileen's

work-basket! How pleased he was! He rummaged in it and looked at her thimble, her needles and pins, her scissors and her cottons.

He liked the needles and the scissors very much indeed. He put the thimble on his head for a hat, and stuffed a packet of needles into his pocket and then picked up the scissors to run off with those, too!

'Those belong to Eileen!' cried the toys, indignantly. 'Give them back at once!'

'Not I!' laughed the goblin rudely. The toys rushed at him, but he danced round and round them, and in and out, punching here and pinching there till the toys were ready to cry with rage!

And then the panda suddenly thought of a perfectly splendid idea! Really splendid! What about Peter's magnet? He rushed to the toy cupboard and poked about for it. At last he found it and brought it out, holding it by the red, curved part.

'What's that you've got?' cried the goblin.

'Something magic!' said the panda. 'It will make you come here to us! You won't be able to go down your mouse-hole to-night!'

'Pooh!' cried the goblin, mockingly.

'I'm not afraid of that silly red thing, so there!'

He danced near to it, and the panda pushed it towards him. And then a

very curious thing happened. The scissors and the needles felt that they must go to the magnet – and as the needles were in the goblin's pocket and the scissors were in his hands, they pulled him to the magnet too! He found himself being taken to that big magnet, and no matter how hard he tried to run away, he couldn't! The magnet pulled him and pulled him, because of the needles and the scissors!

'Ooh! Ow!' cried the goblin, in a

Peter's Big Magnet

fright. 'What is it? What is pulling me? Oh, let me go! It's magic, it's magic!'

The toys laughed to hear the goblin so frightened. The magnet pulled him right up to the panda, and the scissors stuck hard on to it. The needles tried to get out of his pocket too, but they couldn't.

'Seize him!' cried the panda to the toys. The bear caught the goblin by the arms, and the clockwork clown caught him by the waist. He was a prisoner!

The bear tied up his hands, and the dolls tied up his legs.

The panda grinned and put down the magnet.

'Take away from him all the things he has stolen!' he said. So the needles were taken from his pocket, the scissors were put back in the basket, the thimble was pulled off his head. Then his shoes were taken off and given to the doll. His blue tie was pulled away from his neck and the panda tied it once more round his own throat again. The fairy doll took back her brooch and

pinned it joyfully on her frock.

'Now just pay us for the sweets you have stolen!' said the panda fiercely. 'Or we will try our magic on you again!'

The goblin told him to take some pennies out of his pocket. The toys did so, and put them in the sweetshop to pay for the sweets. Then they untied the frightened goblin and chased him to his mouse-hole.

'And if you dare to come back again, we'll have our magic ready for you!' they said. The goblin disappeared with a yell – and that was the very last that the toys saw of him, you may be sure!

They put back Peter's magnet, and danced for joy all round the nursery.

'What will the children say when they find the tiny pennies in the toy sweetshop?' they cried.

Won't Peter and Eileen be surprised? I'd love to be there when they find the goblin pennies, wouldn't you?

12

The Greedy Rabbit

'Let's have a picnic!' cried Loppy, frisking round his mother. 'Do, do, do! There is lettuce to eat, carrots to nibble and turnips too! Mother, let's have a picnic!'

'Very well,' said his mother. 'Go and tell the others, and we'll have a picnic this very afternoon. Ask your friends in the burrow next door too, if you like.'

Loppy bounded off, very happy. He told all his brothers and sisters about the picnic and then they went to ask their friends.

'We'll ask Furry, because she's so sweet and gentle,' said Loppy. 'And Whiskers because he's such fun. And Bobtail because he knows how to play so many games.'

'And Fluff because he's the baby,' said the others. 'But *not* Slippy, because he's so sly and greedy,' said Loppy. 'I don't like him.'

'Neither do we!' cried everyone. So Furry, Whiskers, Bobtail and Fluff were asked – but not Slippy!

Slippy was angry. He watched them all setting off to the picnic, carrying baskets and bags, chattering away happily. He frowned and pulled at his whiskers.

'Nasty things!' he said. 'Horrid mean things! I'd like to spoil their picnic and eat all the things myself! That would just punish them for their meanness to me!'

He sat and thought for a little while – and then an idea came into his sly little head.

'I know! I know! I'll creep under a bush just behind them, when they are having the picnic – and I'll shout out: 'Fox! Fox!' Then they'll all rush off to their holes – and I shall be able to sit down and eat everything by myself. Ho, ho, what a fine trick!'

The sly little rabbit set off after the others. He waited until they were all sitting in a ring, munching carrots, lettuces and turnips, and then he went down a hole, and came up again beneath a bush nearby.

'FOX! FOX!' he yelled. 'FOX! Beware! He is coming. FOX!'

'Oooh! Eeee! Oooh!' squealed the frightened rabbits, and they rushed off down the hill at once, popping into the first holes they saw. The feast was left on the grass – and it wasn't long before Slippy crept out from under the bush and sat down to finish the tit-bits!

He was sitting there very happily indeed, when a sound made him jump. It was the crack of a twig just behind him!

He looked round, his big ears twitching and his nose going up and down in fright.

Tails and whiskers, it was a FOX! Yes – but a *real* one this time! A great red fox with a fine bushy tail sticking out behind him! His sharp nose sniffed Slippy, and he grinned.

'A rabbit!' he said. 'A nice, fat little rabbit – all by himself, and having a grand feast! Ho! What a nice dinner he will make!'

The Greedy Rabbit

The Greedy Rabbit

He pounced – but Slippy was off in a trice, shouting: 'Help! Help!'

But nobody helped him. Everyone had been so frightened when he had called out 'Fox!' before, that now they were all hiding at the bottom of their holes, and not a single rabbit was around to tell him how to escape.

Slippy ran down the hill, and the fox ran after him. Slippy ran under a bush. The fox followed. Slippy tried to get to a hole, but the fox wouldn't let him go near it. Slippy turned and twisted,

151

dodged and dived – but he could *not* get near a hole and go down it. His little heart thumped hard, and he felt sure that he would soon be so tired that he would have to lie down – and then the fox would snap him up!

'Why did I play that mean trick!' he thought. 'Oh, what a punishment this is! Help, help!'

And then a big pheasant, who hated the fox because he had taken her young ones, saw the hunted rabbit. The bird flew to a nearby bush and cried: 'Here come the dogs! Here come the dogs!'

Now the fox was as frightened of the dogs as the rabbits were of the fox – and off he ran at once, his bushy tail streaming out behind him! Slippy sank down, trembling. In a few moments rabbits popped up their heads, and the pheasant told them all that had happened.

'It was my fault!' said Slippy. 'I spoilt the picnic by calling 'Fox!' so that I might eat the tit-bits – and when you had all gone, and I was feasting, a fox *really* came – and nearly caught me. It served me right. I'll never, never be greedy or mean again!'

And as he is always asked to every picnic now, I think he must have kept his word!

13

The Untidy Pixie

The pixie Twinks was always in trouble.
She was so dreadfully untidy! She had
buttons off her shoes, hooks off her
dresses, and holes in her stockings and
her gloves. She had an untidy mind too
– she was always leaving her things
about, dropping her handkerchiefs,
and losing her purse.

Now one fine morning, as she was
going along the road, she met Dame

Hurry-By. She was in a great hurry and she called to Twinks.

'Twinks! I want to catch the bus and I haven't time to go home and put this spell in my cupboard first. Will you take it for me?'

'Yes,' said Twinks, and she held out her hand for the tiny spell, which was like a little blue pill.

'Thank you!' said Dame Hurry-By. 'Put it on the third shelf of the cupboard, Twinks. I'll find it there when I come back!'

Twinks went on to the village to do her shopping. She had her basket with her, for she had a lot of things to buy. She had actually made out a list of things she wanted, so she felt rather pleased with herself.

She came to the shops. Now, what was on her list? She looked in the basket for it – it wasn't there. It wasn't in her hand, or in her pockets either. Bother! She must have left it at home! Twinks was cross with herself.

She did her shopping as best she could, trying to remember everything she wanted. Then she went home – and, of course, she quite forgot all about the spell that Dame Hurry-By had asked her to leave on the third shelf of her cupboard!

Well, when Dame Hurry-By got back that afternoon she went straight to the

shelf in the kitchen cupboard and looked for her spell – and it wasn't there! So she ran to Twink's house in a great way. 'Twinks! Twinks!' she cried. 'Where's that spell you said you would leave at my house for me?'

'Oh, my goodness!' said Twinks in dismay. 'I forgot all about it, Dame Hurry-By!'

'Well, please give it to me,' said Dame Hurry-By. 'I want it.'

Twinks stared at Dame Hurry-By and went red.

'Let me see now,' she said, 'wherever

did I put it when you gave it to me?'

'In your basket, I should think,' said Dame Hurry-By. They went to look – but it wasn't there. There was a hole in the basket, and Dame Hurry-By pointed to it.

'It might have fallen out there,' she said. 'Good gracious me, Twinks, why don't you mend the basket? You'll have that hole getting bigger and then half your shopping will fall out!'

'I may have slipped the spell into one of my gloves,' said Twinks. 'I had them on this morning.'

She went to fetch her gloves. Dame

Hurry-By took each one and shook it –
but the spell wasn't there.

'Each of your gloves has two holes
in,' she said severely. 'You should be
ashamed of yourself, Twinks! The spell

would certainly have fallen out of
either of these. Do you think you put
the spell into any of your pockets?'

'Feel,' said Twinks – so Dame Hurry-
By felt – and, will you believe it, there
was a hole in each of Twink's pockets!
Wasn't it dreadful! Dame Hurry-By
looked sterner than ever.

'Well, if you put my spell into any of these pockets it would certainly have been lost,' she said. 'You are the most untidy, careless pixie I have ever met, Twinks!'

Twinks began to cry, but Dame Hurry-By didn't look any less cross.

'It's no use crying,' she said. 'I feel cross because that was a very important spell. Now think hard – is there anywhere else where you might have put that spell of mine?'

'Well, I do sometimes put my hand-kerchief into my stocking to keep it safe when my pockets have holes in,' said Twinks. 'Maybe I put your spell into one.'

So she took off her stockings, and Dame Hurry-By looked through each one – and her frown got even bigger.

'A ladder all down the back of this stocking – and, dear me, three holes in the toe of this one,' she said. 'Do you *ever* do any mending, Twinks?'

'Not often,' said Twinks. 'Oh dear, I'm so sorry about the lost spell. Do forgive me.'

'No – I shan't forgive you,' said Dame Hurry-By. 'It cost a lot of money. You must pay me for it, Twinks.'

'But I haven't any money,' sobbed Twinks. 'I've spent it all on my shopping this morning. I've only got three pennies left in my money-box.'

'Well, what are you going to do?' asked Dame Hurry-By sternly. 'You've got to pay me for that lost spell somehow!'

'Perhaps I'd better come and do a little work for you,' said Twinks. 'I could come every day till you think I've paid for the spell.'

'Very well. Come to-morrow,' said Dame Hurry-By. 'And don't let me see you coming with any buttons off or holes in your stockings, Twinks. I won't have people looking like that in *my* house!'

So Twinks spent the rest of the day mending her clothes, and then the next morning she set off to Dame Hurry-By's house with a big apron rolled up under her arm. Dame Hurry-By set her to work. She had to wash up the

162

breakfast things, and then do the day's washing.

Dame Hurry-By did have sharp eyes! 'Look at this cup!' she said to Twinks. 'It's so badly washed that there is still

some sugar left in it! And look at that plate – you haven't even washed the mustard away!'

Twinks had to do a lot of work again – and Dame Hurry-By was even more particular over the washing! She made Twinks wash some curtains three times before she said they were really clean! And when Twinks tore one she had to mend it as soon as it was ironed. My goodness – things were done at once in

Dame Hurry-By's house, I can tell you!

Twinks grew very neat and clean herself. She was afraid of Dame Hurry-By's sharp eye and sharper tongue, and she looked anxiously each morning before she went to Dame Hurry-By's to see if all her buttons were on, and her dress neat, and her stockings without holes. Soon she grew quite proud of her smart look, for she was a pretty little pixie who had really spoilt herself by being so untidy.

'Do you think I've paid for that lost spell yet?' she asked Dame Hurry-By one morning.

'Yes,' said Dame Hurry-By. 'And I'm going to give you a silver shilling for yourself, because you have got so much better lately. Here it is – put it into your purse and DON'T lose it, Twinks!'

Twinks got out her little purse and opened it - and whatever do you suppose she saw inside? Guess!

Yes - the lost spell! The little pixie had put it there to be safe, when Dame Hurry-By had given it to her a week or two back. It was the only place she hadn't thought of looking in! Silly Twinks!

'Oh, look, Dame Hurry-By!' said Twinks. 'Here's the spell after all! I had it all the time, quite safely! Oh, how foolish I am!'

'Well, you may still be foolish but you are no longer careless and untidy!' said Dame Hurry-By, with a laugh. 'Here is your silver shilling. Run off home now, and don't forget all the things you've learnt from me!'

Twinks hasn't forgotten them yet – you should see her mending her stockings each week, and sewing on buttons! It was a good thing she thought she had lost that spell, wasn't it!

14

Let's Play Worms

There was once a naughty little imp who made his home in a mouse-hole that led into the nursery. His name was Impetty, and he was the greatest tease the toys had ever known.

He would come springing out of the mouse-hole at night and chase the yellow duck till he lost his quack, pull the pink cat's tail till it came loose, and press the teddy-bear's middle till his

growl was almost worn out.

The toys didn't like him at all. But they simply couldn't get rid of him. He didn't mind being teased back. He could run so fast that it wasn't a bit of good chasing him. He hadn't any growl to press in the middle, and he hadn't any key to wind him up – so they couldn't steal his key and make him be quiet that way.

'If only we could find out something he is frightened of,' sighed the long-haired doll.

'He isn't frightened of anything in the world,' said the yellow duck.

'He must be frightened of *some*thing,' said the pink cat. 'I am frightened of dogs.'

168

'And I am frightened of cats,' said the clockwork mouse.

'And I am afraid of the fire,' said the wax sailor-doll. 'I might melt if I were too near.'

'Here comes the imp,' said the pink cat. 'Oh dear! We never get any peace.'

'I wish I could go out to the pond and swim, or waddle about the wet grass outside and look for worms,' said the yellow duck, with a sigh. 'I hate being chased by that nasty imp. Hullo – where's he gone?'

The imp had shot back into his hole in fright! All the toys stared at one another in astonishment. Now whatever in the world could have frightened him? What a funny thing!

'What did we say that could have given him a fright?' said the long-haired doll eagerly. 'Think hard every-one. Who was speaking when he came out?'

'I was,' said the yellow duck. 'I just said I wished I could go to the pond and swim.'

'What else did you say?' asked the clockwork mouse. 'You said something else, I'm sure.'

The yellow duck thought hard. 'Yes,' he said. 'I said I wished I could go and waddle in the grass and look for worms.'

'Worms! Worms!' shouted the teddy-bear. 'That's it! That's what the imp is frightened of! Now all we've got to do is to get lots of worms and wave them at him and he'll never come back again.'

'Don't be so silly, bear,' said the pink cat. 'As if *we* could get worms! *I've* never seen any wriggling about the nursery carpet.'

'And we can't possibly get out of the window into the garden, for it's shut,' said the sailor doll.

'And even if we could get worms we couldn't be so unkind as to wave them about,' said the long-haired doll, who was very tender-hearted. 'Worms indeed! Quite hopeless.'

The teddy-bear looked glum. He sat down on the brick-box and thought hard – and suddenly a grin came over his jolly little face. 'I know!' he cried. 'I know!'

He ran to where Ann and Jerry kept their paint-boxes. He had seen the two children using them the day before. He

opened the lids. Inside the boxes were little tubes out of which the children squeezed the colours they wanted. Teddy had noticed that they came out like worms!

'See!' he shouted, and taking off the top, he squeezed a blue tube hard. Out shot a long blue worm! The toys shrieked – what a surprise – and what fun!

They all rushed up to the paint-boxes. Even the wooden skittles rushed up to get a tube too. They wanted to join in the fun, you may be sure! There was one for everyone – except for the big sailor doll. But what do you think *he* did? He wasn't going to be left out of the fun! He ran to the basin where the taps were, climbed up to the taps, reached up to the shelf where Ann's tooth-paste was, in a big tube – and took that down to join the toys! Goodness! What a lot of worms there would be – paint worms and tooth-paste worms too!

Soon the imp came running out from

his hole again. The toys held their hands behind them, with the tubes of paint and the tooth-paste tube in them. The imp grinned at them. 'Let's play pinch-me-last!' he said.

'No,' said the teddy-bear, 'let's play WORMS!'

He squeezed his tube – out shot a bright red worm! Every one squeezed the tubes they held – and out sprang blue worms, green worms, yellow worms, black worms, and brown worms! And as for the sailor doll's tube of tooth-

174

paste, well, you should have seen the enormous white worm that came out of *that*! It made him squeal in delight!

The imp stared in horror. Worms! And more worms! Gracious, every toy had a worm! They were wagging and wriggling everywhere!

'Ow!' he yelled. 'Ow! Take them away!'

But the toys didn't take them away – no, they rushed at Impetty with their coloured paint worms and he tore off in fright. He jumped up into the basin – slid down the slippery sides – and went down the hole at top speed!

'That's the end of *him*!' said the bear

in delight. 'My, what fun that was! Look at my worm, everybody! It's a good wriggler.'

The nursery was full of worms – and the toys made so much noise that Ann and Jerry woke up and came creeping to see what the noise was. The toys leapt into the cupboard and lay quiet – but they left behind the squeezed paint-tubes, the toothpaste, and the worms – what a mess!

'Just look at that,' said Ann in astonishment. 'Someone's been play-

ing with our paints. I wonder why?'
But they never knew. If you know
Ann and Jerry, you can tell them what
happened - won't they laugh!

15

The Little Horse Tricycle

One fine sunny morning Paul went out
for a ride on his little horse-tricycle. It
was a nice little tricycle – a wooden
horse on three wheels, and it went
along quite fast when Paul pushed the
pedals up and down with his feet.

Paul called the horse Spotty, because
its wooden coat was painted with big,
black and grey spots. It was getting

rather old, and, one day, its long black tail had come out, which made Paul sad. A horse without a tail looks so strange. Paul tried to stick the tail back, but it all fell to pieces, and he had to throw it away. It was a great pity.

On this sunshiny morning, Paul thought he would ride to Bluebell Wood. So off he went, pedalling down the road and then along the green path into the wood. And it was there that his strange and exciting adventure began!

As he went down the path he suddenly came to a part of the wood he didn't know at all. Queer, crooked little

179

houses stood in a twisty street, and there was a large-windowed shop in the middle, with the strangest bottles of sweets, the queerest cakes and funniest buns he had ever seen. Paul stopped Spotty, his horse, and looked in at the window.

Then things began to happen. A pixie, with long pointed ears, rushed up, went into the shop, snatched up a bottle of sweets and a big chocolate cake, and then ran straight out again.

The shopkeeper at once appeared at the door. and shouted loudly: 'Stop

thief, stop thief! You haven't paid me!'

But the pixie with the pointed ears ran off down the street as fast as ever he could. The shopkeeper, who was a gnome with a red and yellow tunic buttoned up to his throat, danced about in rage – and then he suddenly saw Paul there, staring in surprise, sitting on his little horse-tricycle.

'After him, after him!' shouted the shopkeeper, at once. 'Go on, boy, go after him and catch him!'

The gnome jumped on to the horse behind Paul, and pushed off. Spotty the horse began to go fast, and Paul's feet flew up and down on the pedals. His hair blew out, and he gasped for breath. Spotty had never, never gone so fast before!

'There he is, the thief!' shouted the gnome shopkeeper, and he pointed ahead. Paul saw the pixie running down a hill in front of them, still carrying the bottle and the cake. On flew the horse-tricycle, faster than ever before, down the hill, and Paul began

to feel quite frightened.

'Don't you think we're going rather fast?' he cried to the gnome. 'Suppose we have an accident!'

'Oh, never mind about a little thing like that!' cried the gnome. 'Go on, faster, faster, faster!'

They rushed on, down the hill and up

another. The pixie in front could run really very fast indeed. Paul felt quite surprised when he saw his legs twinkling in and out. He had never seen anyone run so fast before!

Suddenly they came to a big town. It was a strange town, for all the buildings looked as if they were built of wooden toy bricks. The trees had round, wooden stands, just like toy farmhouse trees, and Paul thought they would fall over at a touch!

The runaway pixie rushed down the middle of the street. There was a small pond at the bottom, on which white toy ducks were swimming. The pixie suddenly tripped over a stone and fell sideways, splash! into the pond. The chocolate cake disappeared into the

water and the bottle of sweets fell to the ground and smashed into a hundred pieces.

A wooden policeman suddenly appeared and ran to pull the pixie out of the water. Then up came Paul and the gnome on the wooden horse-tricycle, and, in their excitement, they ran straight into the pond!

They knocked the policeman and the pixie flat into the water, Paul fell in with a splash, the horse rolled on to its head and stuck there with its three

wheels in the air, and the gnome slid into the mud at the edge of the pond and sat there looking most surprised.

Paul climbed out and began to laugh. He really couldn't help it, everyone looked so funny. Then, up came some more policemen, and dragged everyone out, the horse-tricycle too.

'Now then, what's all this?' said the biggest policeman of the lot, taking out a large notebook.

The gnome brushed the mud off himself and explained about the robber-pixie, and how Paul had been kind enough to go after him on his tricycle. The pixie began to cry and was marched off between two of the policemen.

Paul looked in dismay at his horse-tricycle. It was very muddy and very wet. He himself was the same. Whatever would his mother say when he went home?

The gnome saw him looking unhappy and patted him gently. 'Don't worry,' he said. 'I'll take you to my aunt's. She lives nearby, and she will dry our

clothes for us and brush off all the mud. As for your tricycle, don't worry about that either. I'll take it to a shop I know here and they will clean it up beautifully for you.'

'I'll take it,' said one of the police-men. 'I pass by the shop.'

So off he went, wheeling the tricycle, and the gnome took Paul to a crooked little house not far away, where his aunt, a gnome just like himself, lived. She was dressed in red and yellow, with a big green shawl over her head,

and had the kindest smile Paul had ever seen. She listened to the gnome's story in surprise, and then made them take off their wet, muddy things. She wrapped them up in two old coats and sat them by her kitchen fire, whilst she dried their clothes.

She gave them ginger buns and hot cocoa, and Paul enjoyed it all very much. It was most exciting to sit in Toytown with an old gnome aunt

fussing over him, and a gnome shop-keeper smiling at him over a steaming cup of cocoa. What an adventure!

Soon, his clothes were dry, and after they had been well brushed, he put them on again. 'Now, what about my tricycle?' he asked. 'It is really time I went home, for my mother will be wondering where I am.'

Just then there came a knock at the door, and, when the gnome's aunt opened it, what a surprise! There stood the policeman with Paul's horse-tricycle, all cleaned up, shining bright – and whatever do you think! The horse had a brand-new, long, curling tail! You can't imagine how fine it looked!

'It's got a new tail!' cried Paul, in delight. 'Oh, how splendid!'

'The man who cleaned it up thought

perhaps it had lost its tail in the pond,'
explained the policeman. 'So he gave it
a new one, in case it had.'

'Please thank him very much,' begged
Paul. 'Are you coming back with me to
your shop, gnome? I really must go
now.'

'Yes, I'll come,' said the gnome, and
slipped on to the horse behind Paul
once more. 'Good-bye, aunt, and thank
you very much!'

Paul called out the same and off they
went through the crooked streets of
Toytown. When they came to the
gnome's shop he went inside and came
out with a bag of little toffee-sweets
which he gave to Paul.

'Thank you for your help,' he said.
'Come and see me again some day.
Follow that green path and it will take
you out of the wood. Good-bye!'

Off went Paul, full of delight. A bag
of sweets, a new tail for his horse – and
a fine adventure to tell! What a lucky
boy he was!

When he got home he told his mother

all about his adventure in the wood, and at first she smiled and wouldn't believe him. But when she saw the splendid new tail on the horse, and tasted one of the gnome's toffee-sweets, she changed her mind.

'Well, it *must* be true!' she said. 'How exciting for you, Paul! Do let's go and see the gnome one day soon.'

So they are going next Wednesday – and I wish I was going too, don't you?